The Soap Bandit

The Soap Bandit

BY

DENNIS HASELEY

ILLUSTRATED BY JANE CHAMBLESS-RIGIE

Frederick Warne   New York   London

To My Father
—D.H.

For my brother John Andrew
and in loving memory of Ruth Schloss
—J.A.C.R.

Text Copyright © 1984 by Dennis Haseley.
Illustrations copyright © 1984 by Jane Chambless-Rigie.

LIBRARY OF CONGRESS CATALOGING IN PUBLICATION DATA
Haseley, Dennis.   The soap bandit.
Summary: With one stealthy sweep of a town that
has no children, the soap bandit undoes the citizens' preoccupation with cleanliness during the summer
that seven-year-old Jesse visits his aunt.
[1. Cleanliness—Fiction]   I. Chambless-Rigie, Jane, ill.
II. Title.
P27.H2688S0 1983   [E]   82-13434
ISBN 0-7232-6216-0

Frederick Warne & Co., Inc., New York, New York

Printed in the U.S.A. by Holyoke Lithograph Co.
Book design by Barbara DuPree Knowles.

1   2   3   4   5   88   87   86   85   84

The summer Jesse was seven years old
he went to stay with his aunt.
She lived in a town by the sea.
She wasn't used to kids.
There were no kids in that whole town.

No one played in the water or ran on the beaches.
What they would do, the men in their clean white suits
and the women in their starched yellow dresses,
was sit in the shade and drink tea.
Sometimes they'd take a stroll.
And every night they took a bath.
They never seemed to laugh.
And they never got dirty.

Jesse could tell he wasn't
supposed to do these things either,
but somehow he always got dirty.

The first week he was there
his aunt took him to a fancy restaurant.
The waiters marched around in long white jackets
carrying silver trays piled high with food.
Just after Jesse's aunt said,
"Stop playing with your spoon, or you'll make a mess,"
Jesse accidentally spilled a bowl of chocolate pudding
on the clean white tablecloth,
and some dribbled down on his right knee.
Everyone in the restaurant stared.

His aunt wouldn't look at him all the way home.
When they got to her house she made him take a bath.
Jesse sat all alone in the tub with a bar of pink soap.

The second week he was there
his aunt took him
to the town's big meeting
to hear the mayor give a speech.

The town band was standing in a line with shining instruments.
The town policemen were waiting at attention by their
white horses, wearing medals that shone like mirrors.
Jesse's aunt was sitting in a folding chair, by the women in their
starched yellow dresses, and the men in their clean white suits.
And Jesse was practicing walking around the rim
of the town's white fountain.

Just when the mayor was finishing his speech
and everyone was politely clapping,
Jesse lost his balance and fell in that fountain
with a splash.
Everyone in the town stared.
Jesse crawled out all dirty.

His aunt wouldn't speak to him all the way home.
When they got to her house she made him take a bath.
Jesse sat in the tub a long time
and watched the moon rise outside the window
like a big piece of white soap.

And there were other days he got dirty.
When he went walking on the beach
and the waves would set him running,
or walking near the woods
and the trees would reach down their limbs
for him to climb them.
And he would.
And then in the evening he would walk back
through the town to his aunt's house,
past everyone,
looking dirty.

And it was on one of those nights
when his aunt ordered him to take a bath
and he was in his room just starting to take off his clothes
that the soap bandit entered the town.
While Jesse was pulling off his socks
the soap bandit rode through the dark streets on his cart
pulled by his funny horse named Horace
and he tiptoed into all the houses of the men in white suits
and the ladies in yellow dresses
while they sat sipping tea,
and he snuck into their bathrooms
and he took their white and yellow soap
and he carried it out and put it on the cart
that Horace pulled.

And while Jesse was taking off his shirt
the soap bandit snuck into all the shops of all the shopkeepers
and he reached onto their shelves
and he took all their soap, orange and green,
and he carried it out and put it on the cart
that Horace pulled.

And while Jesse was taking off his undershirt
the soap bandit snuck into the mayor's house
while the mayor was giving a speech to his wife
and he took the mayor's soap, which was golden
and shaped like an egg....

And he snuck into the police station
while all the policemen
were brushing their horses
and he took the policemen's soap,
which was blue, like nightfall.

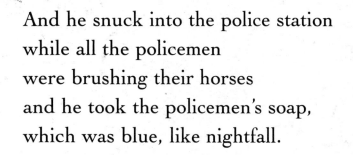

And while Jesse was taking off his pants
and just getting ready to take his bath
the soap bandit snuck into his aunt's house
and he took her pink soap.
And all the soap that he took he piled on the cart
that Horace pulled.
And then the soap bandit rode out of town.

When Jesse walked into the bathroom
and saw there was no soap
he called his aunt and told her
that he couldn't take a bath.
"Impossible," she said,
but she saw that it was true.
And then she told him not to tell anyone else
about their missing soap.
And all over that town
people were discovering the same thing
when they went to take their baths.
And they all said, "Impossible!"
But the soap could not be found,
so no one said a thing,
and all the next day
and the days after that
nobody whispered a word
about the missing soap.

But then, one by one, each on his own,
they started to look for soap.
First they went to the store,
but the soap bandit had been there first.
So they went back to their houses
and looked again through their clean bright rooms,
and when they didn't find any soap there
they looked in other places where they usually didn't go.
They looked in musty attics
and dusty cellars,

and when they found no soap there
they looked in places where they had never been.
Some drove out onto the muddy roads
in their motorcars
past deserted shacks and buildings
looking for old soap factories.

Others went to the library
and quietly took out books on soapmaking
and they went to junkyards and got vats.
They went to butcher shops and got tallow
and late at night they tried to make soap,
but it came out looking like chocolate pudding.

And someone thought he saw a bar of pink soap
floating down a stream
but it was only a fish leaping in the sunset.
And the soap bubbles someone thought she saw
rising toward the sky
were made by a family of frogs, croaking.

And the mayor took a torch
into the town's dark vault

and the leader of the band
searched inside the tubas

and the policemen galloped
on their white horses
kicking up clouds of dust

and stopped to look
for fingerprints and foot tracks
through magnifying glasses
that made their eyes seem big.

They never found any soap,
but whenever someone from the town
saw someone else from the town
he or she would say, "Oh yes, it's a nice day
for driving in a motorcar, or going to the library
or taking a stroll..."
and then they would hurry on
never mentioning at all
that they were looking for soap.

Jesse's aunt
just stayed in her house
drinking tea.
And Jesse
climbed to the tops of the trees
and crawled under rocks
and ran along the shore
looking at everyone
looking for soap
looking at the world....

Weeks went by, and then it was time
for another big meeting of the town.
It was the day for everyone
to stand in the square
and listen to the band
and watch the policemen
and hear the mayor speak.
Everyone was there.
But it was different from ever before....
The policemen were there with their horses,
but the horses were no longer white.
The medals no longer shone like mirrors.
The waiters from the restaurant were there,
but they were no longer neat and fancy.
The band was there, but their uniforms
were soiled, the bright horns dark.
And the men in their suits and the women
in their dresses were there,
but the suits and dresses were no longer
white and yellow.
No one was smiling.
They were all looking down
as if they were feeling bad.

The mayor walked up to the stand
to speak. "Fellow citizens," he said.
And then he stopped.
And he looked at his clothes and hands,
and a smile came to his face.
"Pardon me," he said.
"You see I haven't been this dirty
since I was seven years old...."
And then he looked around the crowd,
at everyone standing there,
and he started to laugh.

And then everyone else — the men and the women, the policemen, the band, and the waiters — looked at each other and they started to laugh. And his aunt looked at Jesse, and he looked at her, and they began to laugh, too....

And that was the moment
the soap bandit
returned to town.
He rode on the cart
pulled by his funny horse named Horace
and it was piled high
with all the soap from the town,
the orange soap and the yellow soap
and the white soap
and the golden soap shaped like an egg
and the soap that was blue like nightfall
and the bar of pink soap...
and the soap bandit
unhitched that cart and left it
right by the fountain.
Then he bowed to everyone
and he got on his horse
and he rode out of town.
and they never saw
him anymore.

But all the rest of the summer
the people of that town
played on the beaches
and ran with Jesse through the waves
and climbed the trees.
And no matter what happened,
Jesse never felt dirty
again.